this book belongs to . . .

_____

To my boys –

Gary, Ryan and Murphy our Bernese Mountain Dog

(the best Critter a family could have)

There's a Pig in my Pantry
by Donna C. McClanahan

Published by HigherLife Development Services, Inc.
400 Fontana Cir.
Building 1 – Suite 105
Oviedo, FL 32765
(407) 563-4806
www.ahigherlife.com

All rights reserved.
ISBN 13: 978-1-935245-65-0
ISBN 10: 1-935245-65-1

First Edition
12 13 14 15 – 9 8 7 6 5 4 3 2 1
Printed in the United States of America

There's a pig in my pantry

donna c. mcclanahan
illustrated by dee deloy

I woke up this morning, to find critters galore
Scampering through my big kitchen door.

What's causing the ruckus? What's causing the stir?
Above all the clamor ...

"Was that a **SN⬤⬤RT** I just heard?"

2

There's a pig in my pantry!

How can this be?

He's pink, rotund, and his tail's SQUIGGLY.

A chef's hat, an apron and orange clogs he wears

I stood there astonished! But he smiles back and stares.

3

Rooting through my cookbooks
I see he's on a mission
Can't he please leave?
That's what I'm wishing!

"What are you doing?
Why are you here?
Are more critters involved?"
I ask with some fear.

"I'm a personal chef,
Hired just for the day.
But I'm behind schedule,

So stay out of **MY** way!"

"A picnic grand, Is what's in store. List my groceries, then out the door"
Well this I can't miss. Yes, this I should see. So I hop in the car, with the cat and piggy.

Old Pork Chop the cat, puts the gas to the floor. I click on my seat belt and *cling to the door.*

The pig in the front seat

Just giggles and squeals

As Pork Chop the cat

Nearly wrecks in the field.

The sirens, they flash,

they whine, they whirl!

The officer approaching is

**Sylvester
the Squirrel**.

Flashing a grin, it's hard to believe,
That he hands me a fine as he heads
out to leave.

"Driving too fast is just for the races.

But you're wearing your seat belts;
So you're in my good graces!"

He tears up the ticket
Just gives a warning,

And we're thankful to leave

With only a scorning.

7

We gathered our treasures
And goodies from the store
Heading back to the house
Me and my critters galore!

Back in my kitchen
We partner to create
A delicious picnic menu

Ahhh, the smells permeate.

There are cakes,
there are pastries,
there's tiramisu,

And even some
caramelly
pretzels too.

The food is packed, The blankets rolled, So much for just one pig To hang on to and hold!

A gaggle of geese Arrive just in time, Helping to carry

These treasures sublime.

To the *lake!* To the lake!

The one in the park

Where we'll dine **al fresco**

Until it gets dark.

We have games we can play

And Lots of good food!

We have music and dancing

And of course the whole crew

Pigs, dogs and cats,

Snakes, squirrels and geese,

Can feel all of their tensions

Start to release.

All involved lend helping hands .
Cooperation is key to our wonderful plan .

"Piggy, we love you!"

We shout , "You're divine!"
The menu is perfection at the hand of the swine .

"Piggy , please stay!" we all insist .
"So we may live together in culinary bliss!"

11

New Words to Learn

Pantry (n): A small room in which food and dishes are kept

Ruckus (n): A disturbing noise

Clamor (n): A loud continuous noise

Rotund (adj): Somewhat round

Permeate (v): To spread throughout

Tiramisu (n): A layered Italian dessert

Sublime (adj): Awesome

Al fresco (adj): Outdoors

Culinary (adj): Related to the kitchen or cooking

RECIPE FOR LIFE
Core Values

Teamwork: **Working in harmony with others**

How do the critters demonstrate teamwork in our story?

How do they mutually benefit?

What's a situation in which you can practice teamwork?

Responsibility: **Being accountable for your own actions**

Which character did not exercise responsibility in our story?

Name a character (or a group of characters) that did act responsibly.

How can you show greater responsibility?

Heavenly Piggy Stix

½ bag of pretzel rods (approximately 18 pretzels)

1 14-ounce bag of traditional caramels

2-3 tsp. water

About 24 ounces pecan halves (or 1 ½ of two 16-ounce bags)

6 ounces Nestle Tollhouse semisweet mini chocolate chips

6 large (1.4-ounce) Heath bars or 18 mini Heath bars

1. Cut candy bars and pecans into chunks and place in a 13 x 9 x 2-inch rectangular pan or glass dish.

2. Add the chocolate chips and stir to combine.

3. In a separate dish, microwave unwrapped caramels with the water for one minute.
   Stir and then cook for another minute. Then stir and cook for another 30 seconds. Let the
   mixture cool slightly.

4. Working quickly, coat ¾ of a pretzel with warm caramel. Roll the pretzel into the pecan, chip and candy
   mixture. Lay pretzel on waxed paper to set. Continue until you have made about 18 pretzels or until the
   toppings are gone.

Note To Parents

Dear Parent or Caregiver,

Our children are a dear gift given to us for a very short time. We must nurture and nourish them and give them back to the world so they can make a difference.

I hope reading to your children will be a bond you forever hold dear. I know it's some of my very best memories with my son!

I also hope The CRITTERS GALORE SERIES will be a fun, interactive way for you to teach your children the Core Values and key character traits that will help them grow up to be responsible and caring individuals.

Here are some simple tips you might consider after reading *There's a Pig In My Pantry* together with your child .

1. Definitely set aside time to make the recipe together. And Please do not be afraid to MAKE A MESS! As this will make a memory! Your child will not remember your clean kitchen. You can also use the time together to discuss the key character traits of of the different animals brought out in this book.

2. Ask your child if they understand what these values mean? Be prepared to share an example of how this character trait was applied in your life, or better yet, point out an example of where you saw your child demonstrate this character trait.

3. Make a chart on your refrigerator or someplace visible where you can give a gold star and write down any time you see your child demonstrate this character trait. You want your child to be able to not only understand the character trait but get into healthy habits of looking for opportunities to express this in daily activity.

All the best,

donna c. mcclanahan

If you'd like to become a member of the Critters Galore Fan Club (It's free!), just go to my website at:

www.mycrittersgalore.com

There you can sign up to receive special pre-publication discounts on the next books coming out in the series.

To have me speak at your group or event feel free to contact me at:

dmc0806@gmail.com

I'd love it if you would write a positive review about *There's a Pig in my Pantry* by posting something both on our website as well as on our Facebook page. Also, feel free to order the book wherever you like to shop for books including: Amazon.com Barnes&Noble.com and other fine bookstore outlets.

You can download the eBook edition of Pigs In My Pantry as well! Feel free to give as gifts to friends and family.

Are You Ready to Have More Fun Adventures Growing in Character?

If you thought Chef Hamsley was fun, wait till you meet the other cast of "Critters" coming soon!

- For Peete Snake teaches the value of Acceptance in There's a Snake from My Lake

- Tammy TuTu and Peppermint Paul are two kangaroos that can teach you Good Manners.

- Babaloo is the Mouse in My House that teaches Sir Julio Mihaly, the gianormous chihuahua to live an active, wholesome life.

- Gorgeous Georges is the Gator in the Garden that teaches you to learn new things without fear.

- Snickers the Wild Boar at My Door teaches about the fellowship of sharing good food, music and conversation with a variety of friends.

- PolkaDot Patty and Lucky Lucca are two turtles that can teach you Perseverance and Self-Belief.

Join all of the Critters as they explore making music and helping Rufus the bear find his potential in the untitled book Co-written with son, Ryan McClanahan.